A 3-D MYSTERY!

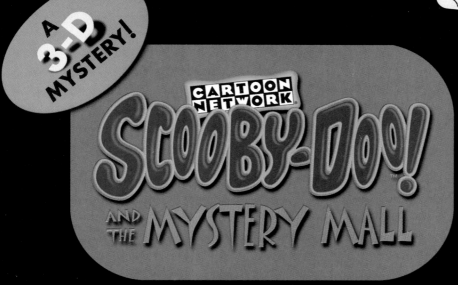

CARTOON NETWORK

SCOOBY-DOO!

AND THE MYSTERY MALL

ISBN 0-590-38656-5

12 11 10 9 8 7 6   8 9/9 0 1 2/0

Special thanks to Arkadia for interior illustrations.

Designed by Joan Ferrigno

Printed in the U.S.A.

First Scholastic printing, September 1998

WB
WORLDWIDE PUBLISHING

SCHOLASTIC INC.
New York   Toronto   London   Auckland   Sydney

Scooby-Doo, Shaggy, Fred, Velma, and Daphne—the gang from Mystery, Inc.—went to a mall. There was a mystery to solve.

"Thieves stole a safe full of rare coins. Other stores have been robbed," the mall security chief explained. "And all the guards quit, because they've seen ghoulish figures floating through the mall at night. Everyone thinks the place is haunted."

"I've never heard of a haunted mall," said Fred.

"Like, I wouldn't mind scaring up some chow at the food court!" Shaggy said. "Get it, Scoob? SCARE up some chow?"

"Ree-hee-hee-hee!" Scooby giggled, although inside he was nervous at the thought of ghouls floating around.

"Jinkies! Look at those tracks." Velma pointed to the ground. "I have a hunch that's our first clue!"

Put on your 3-D glasses and look around. Do you see any other clues?

The gang followed Velma out to the dark loading dock. The security chief returned to his duties.

"I'll bet the thieves put the safe on something with wheels!" Fred exclaimed. "They must have brought it out here for some reason."

"Luckily they tipped over the paint can and provided us with a clue," Velma said. "I wonder where they went next?"

Meanwhile, Shaggy and Scooby got more than they'd bargained for when they went looking for a snack. Suddenly, two ugly ghouls popped out of a box and chased them back into the mall!

When you wear your 3-D glasses, you can see why Shaggy and Scooby were so scared! What else can you see? Where do you think the thieves took the safe?

"Like, usually nothing could chase me out of the food court,
Scoob!" Shaggy cried. "But if anything can, it's a creepy old ghoul!"
"Reah! Rhoul!" Scooby frantically agreed.

Shaggy and Scooby ran through the food court. They wanted to rejoin the rest of the gang, but there were so many signs and arrows, they quickly got lost! And a hideous, floating ghoul was right behind them!

If you put on your 3-D glasses, you can help Shaggy and Scooby find their way out of this mysterious mall maze!

Fred, Daphne, and Velma followed the paint trail into the service elevator. They discovered that the elevator only went down one floor. Soon they found themselves in a dim corridor under the mall.

"This must be how the shopkeepers load their goods into their stores," Velma explained. "I wonder why that door was left open?"

"It looks like someone just abandoned this crate," Fred noted. "What do you think could be in it?"

Daphne looked around. "Hey! What happened to Shaggy and Scooby-Doo? I thought they were right behind us!"

But before the gang could ask any more questions, they were suddenly caught by something from above! They were trapped!

With your 3-D glasses, look at all the clues. What trapped Daphne, Fred, and Velma? What other clues do you see? What do you think they mean?

9

Trying to fool the ghoul, Shaggy and Scooby ducked into a mall fashion boutique. They decided that disguises might just do the trick.

"Like, here, Scoob!" Shaggy said. "Put on this dress."

Scooby shook his head defiantly. "Ruh-uh! Ro way, Raggy!"

"Like, okay, okay!" Shaggy gave in. "I'll wear the dress! Just, whatever you do, don't tell the gang!"

"Ree-hee-hee!" Scooby couldn't help but snicker.

Arm in arm, they casually walked out of the boutique. But the ghoul recognized them when Scooby stopped to scratch—something men in tuxedos rarely do! Not only that, but just then the other ghoul reappeared—making for double trouble!

Put on your 3-D glasses. Do you see a way for Shaggy and Scooby to escape?

Jumping out of their disguises, Shaggy and Scooby hopped aboard a mall security cart and drove away in a flash! With Shaggy behind the wheel, they zoomed through the mall's shops, but the ghouls gained on them.

Inside a sporting goods store, Scooby suddenly yelled, "Rook out, Raggy!"

"I'm trying, Scoob!" Shaggy replied. "But, like, you bring new meaning to the term 'backseat driver'!"

CRASH!

Wearing your 3-D glasses, you can see what was in their path much better than Shaggy could! What was it? What do you think happened next?

Golf balls went flying everywhere! So did Scooby-Doo and Shaggy!
As Shaggy flew through the air, he got another surprise. "Look,
Scoob! Somebody's tied up the rest of the gang and the security chief!"

The golf balls rolled under the ghouls. Instead of gliding over them, the villains started slipping and sliding. Meanwhile, Scooby was about to hit something that would bring down the house!

Put on your 3-D glasses. Can you tell what Scooby hit? What do you suppose happened then?

When Scooby hit the button, the basketballs came tumbling down on the ghouls, knocking them out! The gang unmasked them—it was the twins who own the skate shop!

Velma explained, "I should have known when I spotted this skateboard they used to move the safe. They weren't floating! They were just gliding on skates!"

"The twins were breaking into the other stores at night and taking the stolen goods back to their place." Fred added, "It looks like they were planning to ship the loot out in this crate!"

Daphne smiled. "And they might have gotten away, too, if it weren't for Shaggy and Scooby-Doo!"

"Rooby-rooby-doo!" cheered Scooby.

And you helped solve this mystery with your Scooby-Doo 3-D glasses!